The Curse of the Trouble Dolls

*Here are some other
Redfeather Books from Henry Holt*

*Available in paperback

≈≈≈ Dian Curtis Regan

The Curse of the
TROUBLE
DOLLS

Illustrated by
Michael Chesworth

A Redfeather Book

HENRY HOLT AND COMPANY ▲ NEW YORK

For my father,
who calls after every three chapters
to tell me how he likes the story so far
                    —D.C.R.

Text copyright © 1992 by Dian Curtis Regan
Illustrations copyright © 1992 by Michael Chesworth
All rights reserved, including the right to reproduce
this book or portions thereof in any form.
First edition
Published by Henry Holt and Company, Inc.,
115 West 18th Street, New York, New York 10011.
Published simultaneously in Canada by Fitzhenry & Whiteside Ltd.,
91 Granton Drive, Richmond Hill, Ontario L4B 2N5.

Library of Congress Cataloging-in-Publication Data
Regan, Dian Curtis.
The curse of the trouble dolls / by Dian Curtis Regan;
illustrated by Michael Chesworth.
(A Redfeather book)
Summary: Angie Wu finds herself the center of attention in the
fourth grade when she starts sharing her Guatemalan trouble dolls,
supposedly able to make troubles go away, but then her friends
get mad when the magic does not work for them.
ISBN 0-8050-1944-8
[1. Dolls—Fiction.   2. Schools—Fiction.   3. Chinese Americans—Fiction.]
I. Chesworth, Michael, ill.   II. Title.   III. Series. PZ7.R25854Cu   1992
[Fic]—dc20   91-28572

Henry Holt books are available at special discounts
for bulk purchases for sales promotions, premiums,
fund-raising, or educational use. Special editions
or book excerpts can also be created to specification.

Printed in the United States of America
on acid-free paper. ∞
10 9 8 7 6 5 4 3 2 1

Contents

The Gift

↻↻↻ "I'm home, Mom!" Angie Wu hollered up the narrow stairway as the front door slammed behind her. Mrs. Wu made crafts in a second-floor workroom and sold them to a shop downtown.

"A package for you came in the mail!" her mom hollered back. "It's on the kitchen table."

Angie dumped her book bag into the nearest chair and hurried to the kitchen. Next to a pile of mail sat a small package adorned with colorful stamps.

As she picked it up, her little brother, Willie, dashed into the kitchen. "Let *me* see." He rose to his tiptoes and grabbed for the package.

Angie snatched it from Willie's grasp. He loved to touch everything of hers, and his hands were always sticky.

"It's mine," she said, watching him chew on a gooey

fruit snack. Then she rushed to her bedroom to open the package in private.

Willie followed.

Angie closed the door to keep him out. He was only three, and his sticky fingers hadn't mastered turning slick doorknobs yet.

Her cat, Mimi, was curled in a bright spot of afternoon sun on the carpet. She licked a paw, then sprang onto the bed to see what Angie had brought.

Angie tore the wrapping paper off the package while the cat watched. A note fell into her lap:

Dear Angie,
  Congratulations on starting the fourth grade! Here is a gift from my trip to Guatemala— six Trouble Dolls. Read the instructions carefully and have fun!
                              Love, Aunt Li

Angie pulled off the rest of the paper. Inside was an oval bamboo box small enough to fit into the palm of her hand. Squiggly Indian designs decorated the box.

Opening the lid, she spilled the Trouble Dolls onto her bedspread, counting to make sure all six were there.

The dolls were smaller than Gummi Bears. Angie cupped one in her hand for a closer look. It was made of stiff paper and dressed in bits of cloth and yarn.

The doll's hair was black sand.

Its mouth was a red painted *O*.

Teeny black dots marked its eyes.

Angie showed the doll to Mimi. She sniffed it, then lost interest since it wasn't something to eat.

The doorknob to Angie's room rattled.

"Go away, Willie!" Angie called, sprawling across her bed to play with the dolls. She loved them. "Thank you, Aunt Li," she whispered.

They'd be perfect to show her Reading circle on Sharing Day. She was in the Butterfly group, and when it was her turn to share, she could never think of anything to say.

Angie's best friend, Marybeth Rosario, was a Butterfly too. Marybeth had a broken arm from falling off the monkey bars. She wore a white cast from her hand to her shoulder.

Marybeth always had something to say on Sharing Day. She told the Butterflies about her cast—how the doctor had put it on, how many kids had signed it, and how the doctor planned to saw it off after her bone healed.

The Butterflies had heard the story six times in a row. Only Marybeth told it in a different order each time. Angie thought it was clever of her friend to make one story last for six Sharing Days.

Now Angie had something to talk about too. She could hardly wait until tomorrow.

What should she say? Angie had a million questions about the dolls, but all she knew was printed on a tiny card in the bottom of the box.

It said:

A TEACHING FROM

THE MAYA INDIANS IN GUATEMALA

Take one doll from the box every night for each of your troubles.

While you sleep, the dolls will make your troubles go away.

Limit: six troubles per night.

As she dropped the dolls back into the bamboo box, Angie thought about one of her troubles: Thaddeus Swenson.

Every morning when it was time for the Butterflies

to meet, Thaddeus grabbed the chair right next to hers. Then he smiled a sappy smile and whispered, "I love you, Angie Wu," so only she could hear.

Being loved by Thaddeus Swenson was like being loved by an underfed, scraggly mutt with glasses.

Angie shook one doll from the box. It was a boy doll dressed in brown overalls and a tan shirt.

A tiny voice inside her mind said, "You're silly, Angie. It's only a game. How can a lump of paper and cloth be magic?"

A bigger voice said, "Why not? It's worth a try."

She knee-walked across her bedspread to the dresser, leaned the doll against the lamp, and folded a Kleenex over it for a blanket.

Then she whispered her trouble to the Trouble Doll: "Please don't let Thaddeus sit next to me tomorrow."

Sharing Day

"Today is Sharing Day," Marybeth reminded Angie as they walked to school the next morning. The air was frosty. Ice on the sidewalk shimmered in the light, as if daring the sun to melt it.

"I know." Angie zipped her jacket all the way over her chin.

"Did you think up something to talk about?" Marybeth asked. She wore a red plaid cape, borrowed from her cousin since she couldn't get her cast through the sleeve of her winter coat. It made her look like a Scottish vampire.

"Yep." Angie grinned, touching the bamboo box in her jacket pocket to make sure the Trouble Dolls were there.

"You did?" Marybeth bugged out her eyes. "You *never* have anything to talk about."

"Today I do."

"Tell me now so I don't have to wait."

Sometimes Marybeth acted as impatient as Willie. "It's supposed to be a surprise," Angie told her.

Marybeth thrust her lower jaw forward. "Then give me a hint."

"Well . . ." Angie hopped over an icy curb, trying to make up a good hint. "Remember my aunt Li? The one who travels a lot?"

"The one who sent you the rings all the way from Hong Kong?"

"Yes. Well, my aunt's on another trip, and what I brought for Sharing Day is something she sent me."

Marybeth swirled her cape, tossing one edge across her left shoulder like a real vampire. "Show it to me."

Angie was afraid to open the bamboo box with her bulky gloves. She'd probably drop one of the dolls in a wet puddle and ruin it. "No," she said.

"I'll tell you what *I'm* going to talk about."

Angie chuckled. "I already know what you're going to talk about."

"How could you possibly know?" Marybeth faked surprise as she pulled the cape away, holding her cast high like a trophy.

"Lucky guess," Angie said, laughing with Marybeth at her silliness.

❧

At school, Angie could hardly wait for her teacher, Mr. Nash, to call Reading groups so she could show Aunt Li's gift to the Butterflies. But before he called groups, Mr. Nash gave the class a new assignment and made them copy his directions from the board:

1. Pick a topic to write about.

2. Go to the library and look it up.

3. Take good notes.

4. In class on Friday, write a report using only your notes.

Angie wasn't paying much attention as she copied the directions. She kept practicing her speech for Sharing Time and peeking into her desk at the Trouble Dolls.

Finally it was time for the Butterflies to meet. Angie was so busy moving chairs for her Reading group, at first she didn't notice that Thaddeus Swenson was *not* sitting next to her.

When Angie finally spotted him on the other side of

the circle, her heart thumped-thumped. The Trouble Doll had worked!

Thaddeus stared at her from across the circle.

He smiled his sappy smile.

But he was too far away to whisper, "I love you, Angie Wu."

Suddenly Marybeth jabbed her cast into Angie's ribs. "You're first," she hissed. "Hurry up."

Angie opened the bamboo box and dumped the Trouble Dolls into her hand. Then she walked around the circle, showing them to the Butterflies.

Everyone leaned forward to look at the dolls as Angie told the ancient Indian legend. No one squirmed or whispered.

Kids from the other Reading groups, the Spiders and the Grasshoppers, stopped their seatwork to listen to her story.

Angie's face grew warm. Even Brooke and Ginger, two Grasshopper girls who never paid any attention to her, watched and listened.

Angie's hand trembled as she returned the dolls to their bamboo box.

"Can I hold one?" asked Matthew Tallerico.

"Yeah," came a few other voices. "Pass the dolls around so we can see them better."

But instead Angie shoved the box deep into her

pocket for safekeeping. She didn't mind if anyone looked at her dolls, but she didn't want anyone *touching* them. The magic—if there was any—might rub off.

"Um," Angie stalled, glancing at Mr. Nash. "I think my time is up."

Mr. Nash nodded. "You can answer one more question."

Marybeth's arm shot up. The arm with the cast on it. "Do Trouble Dolls *really* work?" She tilted her head and squinted one eye to let Angie know she was skeptical, even if no one else was.

But Angie knew her best friend well enough to tell that Marybeth was miffed about not getting to peek at the dolls on the way to school.

"Oh, yes!" Angie exclaimed, feeling a sudden need to defend her dolls at all cost. "The Trouble Dolls really, *really* work."

She glanced at Thaddeus Swenson as silent proof.

Planets

After Reading, the class went to the library to begin the new assignment Mr. Nash had given them.

Angie chose planets for her topic. Willie had a planet poster on the wall in his bedroom. Maybe the poster would have good information she could use in her paper on Friday.

Walking along a row of encyclopedias, she searched through the books for the *P* volume.

But her curiosity about Trouble Dolls made her pull out the *G* volume instead. Angie sat at an empty table and opened the book to an article on Guatemala. For the rest of library time, she read about the small country in Central America.

She learned that there are many volcanoes in Guatemala.

She learned that a *quetzal* is both Guatemalan

money and the name of a bird whose picture is on the coin.

She learned about *palo voladare*, the flying-pole dance that's performed at Christmas celebrations in Guatemala.

She didn't learn *anything* about Trouble Dolls.

After school, Angie and Marybeth started for home. The air seemed colder now. Rain, mixed with tiny pieces of ice, fell from a charcoal sky.

Marybeth opened an umbrella and held it high. "Can I ask a favor?"

"Sure." Angie ducked under the umbrella.

"Lend me a Trouble Doll," Marybeth said. "I have to go to the doctor in the morning. Maybe if I tell the doll about my broken arm tonight, the doctor will take off my cast."

Angie hadn't planned on sharing her dolls with anyone. But Marybeth *was* her best friend.

Besides, it surprised her that Marybeth wanted the cast taken off at all. True, it had gotten dirty, and some of the names were so smeared you couldn't read them anymore. Still, Angie figured Marybeth would wear it forever and ever so she'd always have a speech for Sharing Day.

"Please?" Marybeth pleaded. Her nose was as red as her cape from the cold, and she was beginning to get the sniffles. She looked so forlorn, Angie gave in.

Pulling the bamboo box from her pocket, Angie opened it close to her chest so it wouldn't get wet. Yanking off one glove, she picked out a girl doll in a green-and-yellow dress, tied in the middle with a red string.

Giving the doll to Marybeth was hard. Angie sighed as she dropped it into her friend's hand.

"Thanks!" The doll disappeared under the vampire cape.

A beeping horn drew their attention. Mrs. Rosario's car pulled up beside them.

"Oh, I forgot." Marybeth jerked the umbrella away and collapsed it. "My mom is picking me up because we're going to my grandmother's for dinner." She dashed toward the car, yelling good-bye.

Angie shivered in the cold, wishing *she* had a ride home. As she started to put the bamboo box away, Matthew Tallerico rushed up and thrust out a gloved hand.

"I need a Trouble Doll," he insisted. "My mom is having a baby, and I want a brother—not a sister."

Angie wrinkled her nose at Matthew. "I'm not lending my dolls to anyone."

"You are too. I saw you give one to Marybeth." Matthew flicked wet hair from his face with one hand while the other hand stayed, palm up, waiting for a Trouble Doll.

"Marybeth is my best friend."

"So? I've known you longer."

It was true. She'd known Matthew since kindergarten. Marybeth had moved here in first grade. Angie couldn't think of a good answer, so she opened the box once more and chose a boy doll dressed in blue trousers and a ruffly pink shirt.

She watched Matthew's glove fold around it. Now there were only four dolls. Angie was glad she didn't have many troubles.

"Thanks!" Matthew grinned at her, then darted off toward the bike rack.

"Hey!" two voices called.

Turning, she saw Brooke and Ginger waving wildly in her direction.

Angie glanced the other way. Were they waving at someone else?

"Angie!" they both yelled.

She was surprised they even remembered her name. Yet she knew what they wanted. They wanted to borrow Trouble Dolls.

Angie pretended she hadn't heard Brooke and Ginger. Grasping the bamboo box in her fist, she raced through the misty rain for home.

If she wasn't careful, all her dolls would be borrowed away. And she knew what that meant. It meant the dolls would solve everyone's troubles but hers.

Three Down, Three to Go

When she got home, Angie exchanged her wet clothes for a soft pink sweatsuit, then dried her hair with Mom's blow dryer.

Wandering into the workroom, she watched her mother paint tusks on a purple walrus dressed in an apron, holding a chocolate cake in one flipper. Across the bottom of the ceramic sculpture was a banner that read HAPPY BIRTHDAY!

"What is *that*?" Angie watched Mom's quick strokes stipple whiskers across the animal's snout.

"It's a walrus holding a birthday cake." Mom brushed hair from her forehead, leaving a purple streak of paint across her brow. "Like it?" she asked, smiling at Angie.

Angie pursed her lips. "Who would buy a purple walrus?"

"People who collect walruses."

"That's weird."

Mom laughed. "It may be weird, but it's a living. I count on people's hobbies to keep me in business."

Angie looked at the rows of ceramic turtles, dinosaurs, bears, and rhinos lining the shelves. People sure had some strange hobbies.

She watched a few minutes longer, then went downstairs to play with her Trouble Dolls in her bedroom until it was time for dinner. After eating and helping with the dishes, she returned to her dolls.

One was missing.

"Willie!"

Willie wandered into her room. Strawberry jam from his peanut-butter sandwich was smeared red across his cheek like a fresh scar.

"What have you done with my doll?" Angie hoped his fingers hadn't been sticky when he picked it up.

Willie raised his shoulders in a shrug. "I lost it."

"Mom!" Angie yelped.

Mom hurried into the room.

"Willie lost one of my Trouble Dolls."

"Look in his room," she said. "That's where everything lost in this house is finally found."

Angie looked in Willie's room. Zillions of tiny alien dolls, space-hero dolls, and monster dolls were sprinkled across the floor as if a giant battle had raged.

Finding one little Trouble Doll was impossible.

She hurried back to her bedroom, afraid Willie might snatch up another doll if she stayed away too long.

"Did you find it?" Mom asked.

"No." Angie scowled at her brother.

"Willie will find it tomorrow when he helps me clean his room," Mom said, wiping her son's face with the corner of her paint smock. "Won't you, Willie?"

Willie gave Angie a sticky grin. "Dolly, dolly, dolly," he singsonged.

She didn't grin back. Thanks to her pesky little brother, she had only three dolls left.

Angie waited until Mom went back to the kitchen. "Find it," she told him through clenched teeth. "Now."

"Can't." Willie reached to pet Mimi, snoozing on the sofa. His sticky hand came away matted with yellow cat fur.

"Why not?" Angie demanded.

He pointed a stubby finger at his stomach.

Angie gasped. "You mean you *swallowed* it?"

She heard her mother's shriek all the way from the other room.

Before Angie could count to six, Mom had whisked Willie into the kitchen. She sat him on the counter, dialing the doctor with one hand and uncapping a bottle of medicine with the other.

Ugh, Angie thought as she watched Mom prepare her famous concoction. Angie had to swallow the liquid whenever she had a stomachache. And the generous dash of peppermint never eased the agony.

Willie sat stone still, listening to Mom talk to the doctor. The tone of her voice must have scared him, because he started whimpering.

Good, Angie thought. Let him be scared. Let him get what's coming to him.

"Thank you, Dr. Chen." Mom glared at Angie as she hung up the phone. She hadn't cleaned off the paint from her afternoon's work. Now the purple smear on her brow looked like a wrinkly purple frown.

"Lucky for you the doll was made of paper. Dr. Chen says it won't hurt him, but might upset his tummy. This," she said, adding dashes of catnip and ginger to the bottle, "should help."

Willie's eyes grew wide. "Candy?" he asked.

"No, baby," Mom cooed to him. "It's medicine for your tummy."

Willie scrunched his face. "No!" He shoved her arm away.

Angie tried to muster feelings of sympathy for her brother, but it was hard. He'd swallowed her favorite doll—the girl in the fancy amber dress, made from a snip of shimmery satin.

She escaped to another room to get her mind off

Willie's torture session. And her doll. She was quite sure she'd never see it again.

After long minutes of Willie's screams and Mom's loud urging to taste the yummy peppermint, her mother appeared, clutching Willie by one hand as she led him to bed.

Willie looked miserable. His face was as white as Mom's paint smock. It made Angie feel sorry for him after all. But just a little.

"*Please* keep your dolls away from your brother," Mom said, dragging Willie toward the stairway.

"Gladly," Angie muttered to herself, wondering why *she* got into trouble when Willie misbehaved.

Before bed, Angie took a doll from the bamboo box and told it her Thaddeus Swenson trouble. She propped it against the lamp on her dresser.

Taking out a second doll, she placed it next to the first one and told it her Willie trouble: "Please make Willie leave my things alone."

Then she covered them with a Kleenex blanket and sighed.

Half her dolls were gone.

"Oh, well," Angie said to her cat as she climbed into bed. "No need to worry. I never have *that* many troubles all at once."

Mimi gave her a doubtful look.

The Magic Works

⇄⇄⇄ As Angie walked to school the next morning, Matthew sped past on his bike. Icy slush sprayed in an arc from his back tire. "I got a new baby brother!" he yelled.

Angie acted like she wasn't surprised. Yet she was. Sure, she'd told everyone else the Trouble Dolls worked, but she herself didn't quite believe it. Could it really be true?

When it was time for the Butterflies to meet, Thaddeus Swenson did not grab the chair next to hers. Score two for the dolls.

Marybeth arrived in the middle of the morning because of her doctor's appointment. The cast was gone. All the Butterflies crowded around to see her skinny bare arm.

Angie peeked over everyone's head to confirm that

Marybeth's cast was truly gone. "Wow," she whispered to herself, "they really do work!"

Thaddeus fetched a chair for Marybeth. He put it next to his own in the Butterfly circle. Then he grinned at her, making a big fuss over her castless arm.

Angie looked the other way. She didn't care what Thaddeus Swenson did or who he sat next to.

When Reading was over, it was time for class to go to the library. Mr. Nash helped Angie find a book about planets for Friday's paper.

But she didn't read it.

While Mr. Nash was helping someone else, Angie found a book about the Maya Indians and read it instead.

She learned that entire families lived together in mud huts with thatched roofs.

She learned that they made books from fig-tree bark.

And she learned that the Mayas knew an awful lot about the stars.

She didn't learn *anything* about Trouble Dolls.

Marybeth and Matthew kept Angie's dolls.

Angie wasn't pleased about it, but Marybeth had a soccer game she hoped to win, and Matthew wanted to make an *A* on his spelling test.

All afternoon Angie dodged Brooke and Ginger.

They seemed to be following her everywhere, waiting until she took the Trouble Dolls out of her pocket so they could pounce on her.

At recess they pounced, cornering her by the frozen water fountain.

"We want to borrow Trouble Dolls," Brooke said, shaking her head so her wavy blond hair swished back and forth.

"Or else," added Ginger, shaking her head like Brooke—even though her hair wasn't blond, or wavy, or long enough to swish.

"No." Angie crossed her arms, wondering what Ginger meant by "or else." The dolls belonged to her. She didn't have to share them with anyone if she didn't want to.

"You gave one to Marybeth," Brooke snipped.

"She's my best friend," Angie replied, trying the same logic she had used on Matthew.

"You gave one to Matthew," Ginger blurted, imitating Brooke's snippiness.

"I've known him longer." Angie could tell by their blank stares that her logic was failing.

"Well?" Brooke held out an upturned palm. "I have a trouble only a Trouble Doll can solve."

"Me too." Ginger turned her palm up next to Brooke's.

Angie hesitated. It was the first time in her whole life the two had ever paid any attention to her.

"My birthday is next week," Brooke added, touching Angie's arm. "If you give us Trouble Dolls, I'll invite you to my birthday party."

"And," Ginger leaned to whisper into Angie's ear, "if you *don't* give us Trouble Dolls, she *won't* invite you to her birthday party."

Angie wondered if that was the "or else" Ginger had meant. She cupped her hand around the bamboo box. It might be fun to go to Brooke's birthday party. Maybe lending them a doll wouldn't matter so much.

"Will you invite Marybeth to your party too?"

Brooke shrugged. "Sure, why not?"

Ginger raised her eyebrows at Brooke, acting shocked at not being consulted first.

"Okay," Angie told them. "But I can give you only one doll. You'll have to share."

"That's not fair." Brooke's face turned pink. "You—"

"It's okay," Angie said, interrupting her. "The doll can handle more than one trouble at a time." She gave them a girl doll in a white dress, tied with a lavender string.

"Are you sure the doll can handle more than one trouble a night?" Ginger asked, cocking her head to

one side like Mr. Nash did when he asked them test questions.

"Of course," Angie replied, though she wasn't really sure. The card in the bottom of the box had read: "Take one doll from the box for each of your troubles."

But it might work. And it was certainly worth a try if lending a doll would make Brooke and Ginger friendly, and get her and Marybeth invited to Brooke's birthday party.

Angie tried not to think about what else it meant.

It meant she was now down to *two* Trouble Dolls.

Thaddeus Swenson's Secret Trouble

After school, Mrs. Wu drove Angie downtown to the public library so she could research planets for Friday's paper.

Angie liked using the computers at the library. She typed the letters P-L-A-N-E-T-S, then waited for the screen to print a list of titles.

Finding the books, she sat at a table and began to read. But every other minute, her mind wandered back to the Trouble Dolls and all the trouble she was having with them.

Angie glanced at the librarian, Mr. Mullin. Librarians knew lots of things because they read lots of books. Maybe Mr. Mullin knew about Trouble Dolls.

Stepping up to the checkout desk, she waited for her turn to talk to him. She liked Mr. Mullin because he always remembered her name. He'd even bought one of Mom's creations—a calico cat sitting in a chair, reading a book called *Puss in Boots*. Angie spotted it on a shelf behind the checkout desk.

"Angie Wu, how are you?"

That's how Mr. Mullin always greeted her.

She thrust out her hand, showing him the Trouble Doll. "It's a present from my aunt Li," she told him. "Do you know how it works?"

"Hmmm." Mr. Mullin studied the doll. "I don't know anything about Trouble Dolls, but I *do* know how you can find out." He led her to the nonfiction section of the library, then selected a book called *Customs of the Guatemalan Maya*.

Angie carried the book back to her table, shoved aside the books on planets, and read Mr. Mullin's book instead.

She learned that the Maya Indians raised honeybees.

She learned about their sun god, Kinich Ahau, and their moon goddess, Ix Chel.

And she learned that the Mayas abandoned their great stone cities, but no one knows why they left or where they went.

She didn't learn *anything* about Trouble Dolls.

While Angie was reading, someone sat next to her at the table. It was Thaddeus Swenson. He was clutching a stack of books about dragons. Angie guessed dragons were the topic of his report.

"Angie," he whispered. "May I borrow one of your dolls? I have a trouble."

Angie couldn't tell Thaddeus she didn't have any dolls with her. The one she'd shown Mr. Mullin was sitting right in front of her on top of a book called *Planets and You*.

"Sure," Angie mumbled. She watched Thaddeus snatch her doll away and hide it in his fist. "So, what's your trouble?" she asked.

"It's a secret," he whispered.

Angie knew what his secret trouble was. The next time he smiled his sappy smile and whispered "I love you, Angie Wu," he wanted her to smile back at him and whisper, "I love you too, Thaddeus Swenson."

He was probably going to try it right now. She tipped back her chair, crossed her arms, and waited for him to say "I love you."

But Thaddeus didn't say anything. He was too busy holding the Trouble Doll close to his glasses and peering at it. Angie had given him a boy doll dressed in black pants and a plum-colored shirt.

She wiggled her foot back and forth impatiently. Well? Wasn't he going to say it? *I love you, Angie Wu?*

She tapped her pencil point on the tabletop, trying to draw his attention away from the doll.

Still he said nothing. He didn't even smile his sappy smile.

What was wrong with him? Angie untipped her chair, letting it clunk to the floor. She shot Mr. Mullin a look that meant she was sorry for the noise, then leaned her elbows on the table and tried to read Thaddeus's face.

"Well?" she asked. She'd never had to wait for him to say it before.

Thaddeus pushed up his glasses. He acted annoyed that Angie had disrupted his intense study of the doll. "Well, what?"

Well, she certainly wasn't going to *ask* him to say it.

Angie didn't bother to answer. She slammed Mr. Mullin's book shut to show Thaddeus she didn't care whether he said "I love you" or not.

Carrying the book to the nonfiction shelf, she shoved it into place. Maybe she was wrong about Thaddeus Swenson's secret trouble. Maybe it had nothing to do with her at all.

Maybe it had something to do with Marybeth, instead. *She* was the one he'd been sitting with in the Butterfly group this week.

Angie's neck heated in anger. She returned to the table and gathered her things to leave.

She didn't care *what* Thaddeus Swenson's secret trouble was, because now—thanks to him—she had only *one* Trouble Doll left.

All Gone

𑀼𑀼𑀼 When Angie got home, she rushed to her room to check on her last Trouble Doll. She'd left it on top of the dresser—too high for Willie to see if he wandered into her room.

The doll was gone.

"Willie!" she screamed.

Willie came running.

"How could you touch my doll after what happened last night?" She wondered if he'd climbed onto her bed so he could reach the top of the dresser.

"I didn't touch it."

It was then Angie noticed that Willie was licking the side of a gooey root-beer Popsicle. It was melting. Sticky brown Popsicle drops were falling onto the carpet.

"Get out of my room! You're making a mess!"

Angie rubbed one of the spots with her shoe. Now she'd be in trouble with Mom. Willie wasn't allowed out of the kitchen when he was having his afternoon snack.

"You *called* me."

"I know. I know. Get going." She hopped over the gooey mess and pushed him out the door.

Willie walked backward down the hall, holding the Popsicle above his head. Sticky rivers trickled down his bare arm.

He backed into his mother.

"Willie!" Mom grabbed Willie's other hand and rushed him toward the kitchen.

"I saw it!" he called over his shoulder to Angie.

"You saw what?"

"Dolly."

Mom threw an angry glance at Angie. "I thought you promised to keep your dolls away from Willie."

"I did." Angie was confused. She followed them into the kitchen. "Willie, you told me you didn't take it."

"I didn't."

"Then who did? A ghost?"

"No. Mimi."

"Mimi?" Angie had forgotten that her cat liked to jump on top of the dresser and bat away anything small—like a ring or button or penny. And one Trouble Doll was definitely small.

Angie raced back to her room. Mimi was asleep on the bed, looking fat and innocent.

Angie dropped to her hands and knees and crawled around the bedroom floor, looking for the doll. No luck. Why hadn't she put it back into its bamboo box?

She searched her room until dinnertime. After dinner she searched until bedtime. Still no doll.

Climbing under the covers, Angie shook one finger at Mimi so she'd know her master was angry with her. Purring anyway, the cat nestled against Angie's shoulder.

Angie closed her eyes to sleep. But she couldn't. Panic seeped into every dream. All her Trouble Dolls were gone.

❀

The minute Angie stepped into her classroom the next morning, she knew something was wrong.

Brooke and Ginger huddled in one corner, whispering. Angie had a funny feeling they were whispering about her—mainly because they were pointing in her direction.

Marybeth arrived and glowered at her. "Well," she began in a crabby voice as she slid into the desk behind Angie, "we lost."

"Lost what?"

"My soccer team lost our game last night."

Angie didn't know what Marybeth was talking about. Then she remembered. Marybeth had kept a Trouble Doll so her soccer team would win.

At first Angie was surprised. If Marybeth's team lost, that meant the Trouble Doll hadn't worked.

Then she felt relieved. Maybe now she could get her doll back. She held out her palm so Marybeth could return it.

"Plus," her friend huffed, "look at this!" She held up her right hand. The pinky finger was in a cast the color of raspberry ice cream. "I broke it during the game."

Angie held her breath to keep from laughing. Marybeth was pretending to be mad, but Angie bet she was thrilled to have another cast. Now she'd have something new to talk about on Sharing Day for the next six weeks.

"So," Angie said, still holding out her palm. "I guess you don't need my doll anymore."

Marybeth shifted sideways in her desk and gazed out the window. "I think I lost it."

"What?" Angie couldn't stand the thought of another lost doll.

"Well," Marybeth said, now gazing at the ceiling,

"when my team started to lose, I took the doll out of my pocket so I could hold it in my hand for luck. Then the soccer ball went out of bounds, and I had to throw it in with both hands. That's when I dropped the Trouble Doll."

"Why didn't you pick it up?" Angie asked, resisting the urge to break another one of Marybeth's fingers.

"Because I had to dribble the ball down the field." She gazed out the window again. "I went back for your doll, but by then it had gotten trampled in the mud, and I couldn't find it."

Before Angie could say more, Marybeth looked her straight in the eye. "Don't get mad at *me*," she snapped. "It's all *your* fault. If we'd been winning the game, I wouldn't have taken the doll out of my pocket in the first place."

Angie swallowed hard. She tried to tell herself that four dolls were just as good as six.

"Thanks a lot," came a boy's voice from behind her.

Angie turned. Matthew Tallerico flung his spelling paper onto her desk as if it were too hot to hold. A capital *F* in bright red marker was scrawled across the top.

"You flunked your spelling test," Angie said, wondering again why the Trouble Doll hadn't worked.

"No kidding." Matthew's voice sounded as crabby as Marybeth's.

"Did you study?" she asked.

"I didn't *need* to study. I had a Trouble Doll." Matthew crumpled the paper into a crinkly ball. "Your stupid dolls don't work."

She held out her hand. "Then give it back."

Matthew's expression twisted from anger to guilt. "I don't have your doll."

"Did you leave it at home?"

"No."

"Where is it?"

"I flushed it."

"You *what*?"

"It made me so mad, I flushed it."

The bell rang.

"Still," Matthew snarled as he hurried to his desk, "it's *your* fault that I flunked."

The Curse

卍卍卍 Angie's face burned.

Everyone had lost her dolls!

And they were all blaming *her* for their bad luck. Why didn't they blame the dolls instead? Or the Maya Indians?

She touched the empty bamboo box inside her pocket. Well, three dolls were just as good as six. Maybe. At least she still had Thaddeus's doll, Brooke and Ginger's, and the lost doll at home.

Today's reading assignment was a story about a Chinese emperor's daughter named Mi Sun. It was a fable Angie knew well because her mom had told it to her many times. She pretended to read the words, but in her mind she puzzled over why the dolls had worked for her but not for anyone else.

Maybe the magic was meant for the owner of the dolls, and for other kids it was a curse.

"Terrific," Angie mumbled to herself. "All my friends are being cursed—thanks to me."

At recess Brooke and Ginger followed Angie outside. As much as she hoped they were coming to ask her to play tetherball with them, she had a funny feeling that wasn't why they were stomping up behind her.

"You lied to us," Ginger grumbled. "I had to go to the eye doctor this morning, so I told your Trouble Doll I wanted to get contact lenses. But my mom made me get *glasses*! *Ugly* glasses."

Ginger yanked a pair of glasses from her pocket and shoved them onto her face as though she wanted Angie to see just how ugly they were.

"And," Brooke added, "my dad is looking for a new job, so I asked the Trouble Doll to help him find one. And he did. But it's clear across the country, so now I have to move away!" Brooke sniffled into a flowered hanky.

"Not only that," Ginger hissed, glaring at Angie. "Brooke had to cancel her birthday party because her mom has to go find a new house."

Brooke sniffled louder.

Ginger gave a toss of her head. "She wouldn't have invited *you* to her party anyway."

Sighing, Angie held out her hand so they could return her doll.

"Give it to her." Ginger spat out the words as if getting rid of the doll would make their new troubles go away.

Brooke stopped sniffling. "I thought *you* had it."

"No," Ginger said. "I gave it to you, remember?"

"No you didn't."

Brooke and Ginger forgot about Angie as they argued over who had the doll. Then they wandered off to play tetherball—Ginger pushing up her ugly new glasses, and Brooke crying into her flowered hanky.

Angie sat alone on a brick wall, mourning the loss of her dolls while she waited for the recess bell to ring.

Were two dolls just as good as six?

And was it really her fault everyone was having such bad luck?

No, she told herself. It wasn't her fault. It was the fault of the Trouble Dolls.

Or rather, the *curse* of the Trouble Dolls.

That night Angie climbed into bed and listed her troubles to Mimi. With unblinking golden eyes and perked ears, Mimi seemed concerned.

"Trouble number one," Angie began: "Thaddeus Swenson.

"Trouble number two: Willie.

"Trouble number three: Marybeth and Matthew are mad at me, *and* they both lost my dolls.

"Trouble number four: *You* know where a doll is hidden." She tapped one finger on the cat's white nose. "But you won't tell me."

As she counted again on her fingers, another trouble popped into her mind. Brooke and Ginger. *"Five* troubles!"

Angie pulled the covers to her chin. "Mimi, I need *five* dolls tonight."

She closed her eyes to fret over her troubles. As she started to doze, a thought made her jerk straight up in bed. Mimi yowled and sprang away.

Planets! She'd forgotten about planets!

Tomorrow was Friday, and she wasn't ready to write her report.

Flopping back, Angie yanked a pillow over her head and wailed, "I need all *six* of my dolls tonight!"

Suddenly an idea came to her. She snatched the pillow off her head and hugged it. Maybe she could get

up early in the morning and read about planets in her home encyclopedia before leaving for school.

Then she remembered the planet poster on the wall in Willie's room. If she got up *extra* early, she could tiptoe into his room and copy the drawing of the solar system in her notebook, then label each planet.

A drawing along with her report would really impress Mr. Nash. It was a great idea.

Satisfied, Angie clicked off the lamp on her dresser.

She tried not to notice there were *no* Trouble Dolls sleeping quietly under their Kleenex blanket tonight.

No More Magic

Angie woke up late.

She didn't have time to read about planets in her home encyclopedia before leaving for school. She didn't even have time to tiptoe into Willie's room and copy the drawing of the solar system.

She barely had time to get dressed and eat two bites of breakfast.

Mom stopped what she was doing to drive Angie to school. What she was doing was scrubbing Willie's trail of sticky brown Popsicle spots off the hall carpet. She frowned at Angie all the way to school.

"Hey!" Angie blurted as a crazy idea popped into her head.

"What?" Mom slammed on the brakes. "What's wrong?"

"Have you ever made a planet sculpture?" Angie

felt excited. Maybe Mom could rush home, find a sculpture of the solar system, and dash back to school with it. Then Angie would have something about planets to turn in after all. Maybe not what Mr. Nash wanted, but at least something.

Mom smiled apologetically at the driver behind her, then frowned at her daughter again. "Yes, I've designed several—a bouquet of roses sprouting from a tree trunk, a basket of daffodils, and—"

"No, Mom. Not plants. *Planets*."

Mom raised an eyebrow at her. "Planets? You mean like Jupiter? Pluto? Mars?"

"Yeah." Angie nodded as if she'd asked the most logical question in the solar system.

"No."

"Why not?"

"People collect a lot of strange things, but I've never heard of anyone collecting planets. They're not exactly cute and cuddly."

Angie's last glimmer of hope went swirling down the drain, just like the Trouble Doll she'd lent Matthew.

꙳

When she got to school, Marybeth and Matthew were not speaking to her. Neither were Brooke and Ginger.

Thaddeus Swenson grinned all morning. Angie couldn't tell whether his grins were meant for her or for Marybeth.

He was probably eager for the Butterflies to meet so he could grab the chair next to hers.

Or the chair next to Marybeth's.

Why did it bother her to think of Thaddeus sitting next to Marybeth? After all, Marybeth *was* her best friend.

Angie shook thoughts of Thaddeus Swenson from her mind. She had more important things to worry about right now.

Like her missing Trouble Dolls, and the names of all the planets.

And her best friend not speaking to her, and Matthew and Brooke and Ginger *never* speaking to her again in her lifetime.

And Willie being such a pest, *and* Mom being angry with her.

If only she'd had her Trouble Dolls last night.

"Take out a piece of paper." Mr. Nash's voice startled Angie out of her daydream. "And find the notes from your trips to the library."

Angie slumped in her chair. She didn't *have* any notes from her trips to the library.

Mr. Nash picked up a timer from his desk. "You

have a half hour to write your report," he said, setting the arrow for thirty minutes. "You may begin."

The scribbling of twenty-five pencils sounded loud to Angie as she slowly wrote across the top of her paper:

Planets
by
Angie Wu

Angie stared at the blank page for ten minutes.

She tried to picture the names of all the planets listed in neat columns like they were on Willie's poster. She even tried to sketch the egg-shaped circles showing each planet's orbit around the sun.

She couldn't.

She didn't know anything about planets.

She couldn't even name them all by heart, like Willie. True, she never understood what he was saying when he rattled off all nine names. But still, *he* knew.

Behind her, Angie could hear Marybeth writing fast and dotting her *i*'s hard. Angie glanced over one shoulder. While Marybeth wrote, she held her pinky finger up in the air so everyone could see her raspberry-ice-cream cast.

Angie groaned. Marybeth was probably writing a report called "The History of Casts."

Angie's eyes came back to her own blank paper. She was going to get a big red *F*, just like Matthew got on his spelling test. She could already picture her mother's disappointed look when she saw the grade.

Why had she brought her Trouble Dolls to school in the first place? Why had she lent them away? And why hadn't she kept an eye on them when Willie was around?

Angie laid her head on her desk and closed her eyes. If only she'd had *one* Trouble Doll last night, her planet report would be halfway finished by now.

Who Needs Magic?

卐卐卐 Trouble Dolls!

Angie opened her eyes and shot up straight in her desk. Feeling excited, she pulled out a fresh sheet of paper and wrote across the top:

Guatemalan Maya Indians
by
Angie Wu

Angie's pencil scribbled even faster than Marybeth's as she wrote about Guatemala, the Mayas, and their legends.

She wrote about honeybees and volcanoes.

She wrote about flying-pole dancers and fig-bark books.

She wrote about sun gods and moon goddesses.

She even wrote about Trouble Dolls.

卐

After recess Mr. Nash called Reading groups.

"Angie," he said, smiling, "I haven't had time to grade reports yet, but yours looks quite interesting."

Angie felt embarrassed and pleased at the same time. She hadn't needed help from a Trouble Doll after all. She'd done it on her own.

As a matter of fact, the dolls had *given* her more troubles this week than they'd taken away.

Still, they were a gift from Aunt Li, and they rightfully belonged to Angie. She'd make Thaddeus Swenson give back her doll. And the one Mimi lost at home would turn up sooner or later. Lost toys always did.

Angie sat sideways in her desk and smiled at Marybeth, hoping they could be best friends again. "I like your new cast," she whispered. And she meant it. It was kind of neat the way it permanently crooked Marybeth's little finger.

Marybeth was very, very pleased. "I had my choice of colors—robin's-egg blue, sour-lime green, or raspberry sherbet." She offered Angie a felt-tip pen. "Would you like to sign it?"

Signing a finger cast was a lot harder than signing an arm cast. Angie printed the letters as tiny as she could so there'd be room for other names.

"Angie?" Marybeth whispered. "I'm sorry I lost your Trouble Doll."

Angie gave back the pen. "It's okay." And it was,

because all they'd done was cause trouble between her and Marybeth.

When it was time for the Butterflies to meet, Angie helped move chairs into a circle, then took her seat.

Thaddeus Swenson slid into the chair next to hers, almost tipping it over in his eagerness. Angie couldn't help feeling smug since he'd chosen her to sit with instead of Marybeth.

Thaddeus stared deep into her eyes, as if he were trying to cast a magic spell over her. Then he smiled his sappy smile and whispered, "I love you, Angie Wu," so only she could hear.

Angie watched Thaddeus's eyes widen under his scraggly-mutt hair and glasses. He looked as if he were about to see a ghost as he waited for her to smile back at him and whisper, "I love you too, Thaddeus Swenson."

But she didn't.

A million trillion Trouble Dolls could *not* make her say "I love you" to Thaddeus Swenson.

Still, it was kind of nice hearing him say it again.

She answered by holding out her hand so Thaddeus could drop his borrowed Trouble Doll into it.

The corners of his mouth turned down in disappointment. "Did I do it wrong?" he blurted.

Angie swallowed a laugh. Thaddeus hadn't meant to

let his secret trouble slip out. Now he knew that she knew. "No," she told him. "You did it just right."

Thaddeus stared at her outstretched hand. "I don't have your doll," he said in a tiny voice. He kept his eyes on her hand as if he hoped the doll would magically appear. "I think I lost it," he added.

Anger warmed Angie's cheeks. She curled her hand into a fist and tried to glare at Thaddeus, but her anger cooled as quickly as it had heated up. She really wasn't mad at Thaddeus. She didn't even care how he'd lost her doll. It was a relief not having them to worry over anymore.

Mr. Nash started reading a story about a magic cow. Angie was glad Aunt Li hadn't sent her a magic cow. Imagine how much trouble *that* would've caused on Sharing Day. Besides, how would she have gotten a magic cow into her pocket?

Angie held the empty bamboo box in her hand while Mr. Nash read. The box would be a perfect place to store the rings Aunt Li had sent from her trip to Hong Kong.

Angie smiled as she thought about Aunt Li and the silliness of carrying a magic cow in her pocket.

Thaddeus Swenson, still gazing at her, thought the smile was meant just for him.

So Angie let him think it was.